The Hummingbird Garden

by Christine Widman
illustrations by James Ransome

Macmillan Publishing Company   New York
Maxwell Macmillan Canada   Toronto
Maxwell Macmillan International
New York   Oxford   Singapore   Sydney

Macmillan Publishing Company is part of the Maxwell Communication Group of Companies. Macmillan Publishing Company, 866 Third Avenue, New York, NY 10022. Maxwell Macmillan Canada, Inc., 1200 Eglinton Avenue East, Suite 200, Don Mills, Ontario M3C 3N1. First edition. Printed in the United States of America. The text of this book is set in 14 pt. Berkeley Old Style Book. The illustrations are rendered in oil on paper.

Library of Congress Cataloging-in-Publication Data. Widman, Christine Barker. The hummingbird garden / by Christine Widman ; illustrations by James Ransome. — 1st ed.   p.   cm. Summary: Drawn by the hummingbirds in her neighbor's garden, Jonna comes in for a closer look and makes a new friend. ISBN 0-02-792761-X [1. Gardens—Fiction. 2. Hummingbirds—Fiction.] I. Ransome, James, ill. II. Title. PZ7.W6346Hu 1993   [E]—dc20   91-27338

1 3 5 7 9 10 8 6 4 2

To the memory of my grandmother
and
to Trishia for all the memories
—C. W.

To my loving in-laws, Ernestine and William Cline
—J. R.

It was the time before twilight.

The hummingbird lady rushed out of her house, pushing pins into her wild red hair.

"Oh dear, oh dear," she murmured. "I hope I'm not too late."

She sat down by her garden where bee balm bloomed, and columbines and phlox, tiger lilies, petunias, and four o'clocks. "Come, little birds," she sang out, waving a pink petunia in the air.

Jonna watched her from behind the old fence that separated their yards.

She watched the hummingbird lady call her hummingbirds.

Zumm

zumm

zumm

zumm

On humming wings the hummingbirds flew into the garden.

They hovered above the bee balm and darted among the phlox. They disappeared inside the bells of the lilies and they danced around the hummingbird lady.

But before Jonna could count to ten…*zumm zumm   zumm zumm*…the tiny birds flew away again.

The hummingbird lady stood up and hurried back to her house.

Jonna didn't move. *I wish I were a hummingbird lady,* she thought.

A mourning dove called…*coo ah coo coo coo.* Fireflies twinkled everywhere as if stars had spilled from the evening sky.

Is there magic in that garden? wondered Jonna.
She unlatched the gate…and then…
she slipped inside the hummingbird garden.

The wet grass cooled her bare feet. A breeze blew across her cheek. She smelled the sweet scent of lilies.

Through a lighted window, Jonna could see the hummingbird lady moving about in her house. She looked as if she were inside a glass bottle.

Zumm zumm   zumm zumm
What was that?
Something was hovering by a flower.
Jonna tiptoed close.
Zumm zumm   zumm zumm
Was it a hummingbird?
She tiptoed closer.

Clunk.

Jonna tripped over a flower pot.

Cre-ea-k.

The hummingbird lady opened her door.

"Who's in my garden?" she called out.

"I am," said Jonna, stepping into the light of the porch lamp. "And I think a hummingbird is here, too."

"Hmmm…" the lady murmured. "How odd. Hummingbirds are in their nests at night."

Zumm zumm   zumm zumm

"Look!" cried Jonna. "Here it comes."

A giant moth with wings like dust fluttered up to the porch lamp.

"Why, that's not a hummingbird," said Jonna.

"No, it's not," said the lady. "But some people call it a hummingbird moth."

Jonna watched the huge moth flap against the glass globe. "It wants to go back to the garden," she said.

"Yes, it does," whispered the lady, turning out the light. "Shhh."

Zumm zumm   zumm zumm

Jonna and the hummingbird lady followed the moth into the garden. It fluttered above the bee balm and flitted among the phlox.

"It's like a dancing shadow," said Jonna.

She looked at the hummingbird lady. "I think there's magic in your garden."

"I think so, too," said the hummingbird lady in a voice as soft as moth wings.

The moon floated up. It was bedtime.

"I have to go now," said Jonna.

"Would you like to come again and watch hummingbirds with me?"

"Yes," said Jonna. "I'll come tomorrow."

"Don't be late," said the hummingbird lady.

Jonna opened the gate and walked the silver moon-path home.

In the garden, the hummingbird moth danced around the bells of the lilies.